S0-APQ-730

John McKinney

Cherry Lake Publishing
Ann Arbor, Michigan

Published in the United States of America by Cherry Lake Publishing
Ann Arbor, MI
www.cherrylakepublishing.com

Content Adviser: Thomas Sawyer, EdD, Professor of Recreation and Sports Management, Indiana State University, Terre Haute, Indiana

Photo Credits: Cover and page 1, © John McKinney; page 7, © Kevin Schafer/Corbis; page 21, © Theo Allofs/zefa/Corbis; page 26, © Michael Pole/Corbis; page 29, © Uli Wiesmeier/zefa/Corbis

Library of Congress Cataloging-in-Publication Data
McKinney, John.
Hiking / by John McKinney.
p. cm.—(Healthy for life)
Includes index.
ISBN-13: 978-1-60279-020-9 (lib.bdg.) 978-1-60279-086-5 (pbk.)
ISBN-10: 1-60279-020-5 (lib. bdg.) 1-60279-086-8 (pbk.)
1. Hiking. 2. Hiking—Health aspects. I. Title. II. Series.

GV199.5.M354 2008
796.51—dc22 2007005076

Cherry Lake Publishing would like to acknowledge the work of The Partnership for 21st Century Skills.
Please visit www.21stcenturyskills.org *for more information.*

Table of Contents

CHAPTER ONE

HITTING THE TRAIL

Hiking takes you into the great outdoors.

Hiking is one of the simplest outdoor activities that people can take part in. It is also one of the most rewarding. Hiking is taking a walk in nature, usually on a trail, just for fun. Walking on sidewalks to school is not hiking, and neither is walking around the mall. But walking a nature trail in Rocky Mountain National Park is hiking. So is walking a path around a pond or a trail through the forest. Every hike is a walk, but not every walk is a hike.

A hike can be a half hour, a half day, or many days long. Some people hike the same trails near where they live over and over again. Others like to explore new trails in mountains far from home. Backpackers are hikers who carry enough gear to camp overnight.

People enjoy hiking because it gets them out in the fresh air and exercising. They like seeing interesting plants and animals along the way. Many people hike because it brings them to quiet and beautiful places. Hiking is a fun outdoor activity you can do your whole life. Even if the **terrain** gets difficult at times, you'll feel proud of yourself once you've accomplished what you set out to do.

Hiking can be a challenge, but it is also rewarding. Nothing is more satisfying than struggling up a hillside, reaching the top, and then looking back down at the incredible feat you just accomplished. To be an effective hiker, you need to take the initiative and set reasonable goals. Which trail should you hike and how far should you go? You may have to really push yourself to achieve your goal. If you are hiking with a group, you may find yourself taking a leadership role. As a leader, you may need to motivate others to brave the trail. If it's just you and a friend on the trail, you can work together and encourage each other.

People around the world enjoy getting out into nature. Here are some of the greatest hiking trails around the globe:

1. West Coast Trail, British Columbia
2. Cornwall Coast Path, England
3. John Muir Trail, California
4. Kalalau Trail, Hawaii
5. McGonagall Pass, Denali National Park, Alaska
6. Fitz Roy Grand Tour, Patagonia, Argentina
7. Kungsleden, Sweden
8. Mount Everest Base Camp Trek, Nepal
9. Mount Kilimanjaro, Tanzania
10. Routeburn Track, New Zealand

Lots of kids like to hike. They hike with their friends, their families, the Girl Scouts, Boy Scouts, and other groups. They hike with their teachers and classmates and with rangers and guides at nature parks. Hiking is one of the most popular kinds of outdoor recreation in America. About one out of every three Americans goes hiking every year. Hiking is also popular in Europe.

Forests, deserts, beaches, hills, mountains, and even city parks are great places to hike. Some hiking trails lead to special places: to waterfalls, to meadows covered in wildflowers, to the top of a mountain and great views, to a pond filled with turtles. Other trails lead to bird-watching spots, swimming holes, picnic areas, and campgrounds.

Hiking trails sometimes lead to magical places.

You don't need to travel far away to go hiking. You might discover wonderful hiking trails in parks and nature preserves close to home.

Hiking allows people to enjoy the great outdoors and get in touch with nature and the surrounding environment. It can also be a great way to learn about the environment and gain a global awareness about the issues that affect it. Have you ever walked down the street and found a piece a litter on the sidewalk? Now imagine that same piece of litter in the midst of a beautiful forest preserve. It stands out more, doesn't it?

Unfortunately, pollution and litter are problems in many wilderness areas. But when you go hiking, you connect with nature. Through hiking, many people begin to develop a sense that it is important to preserve the environment for future generations.

CHAPTER TWO

Getting Ready to Hike

Hiking is easy to get into and doesn't require high-tech equipment. Some outdoor clothing, a pair of hiking boots, and a small backpack are all the gear you need to get started.

The best way to pick clothing for a hike is to understand what hikers call layering. Layering is just what it sounds like: if it's chilly, rather than

Hiking is a simple activity. All you need are sturdy, comfortable shoes and a daypack.

Bring an extra sweater or fleece jacket when you hike. The temperature sometimes varies dramatically on mountains.

wearing one heavy sweater, wear two or three thinner layers. That way, if you get warm, you can remove any or all of the layers of clothing. A good choice when layering is a **fleece** jacket. Fleece looks great, is easy to care for, and keeps you warm. It doesn't weigh much, so when you take it off and stuff it in your pack, it's easy to carry. And if there's any chance of rain, don't forget a rain jacket.

Hiking boots have sturdy soles and good ankle support.

The kind of pants hikers wear depends on the weather. Some hikers prefer lightweight long pants, even in warm weather. Long pants protect the legs from scratches and from the sun's burning rays. Many kids like to wear what they call **zip-off pants**. These are long pants that have zippers above the knee so you can zip off the bottom half, changing them into shorts.

Many hikers also wear hats. Hats are important in cold weather because your body loses heat through your head. And in the summer, they keep you cooler by keeping the sun off your head. A baseball cap is fine, but a hat with a big brim is even better.

The single most important thing you need when you go hiking is a comfortable pair of hiking boots. You'll want boots that fit snugly and support your entire foot and ankle. When you try on hiking boots, make sure that your toes don't touch the front or top of the boot. Many young hikers wear lightweight hiking boots that are like sneakers with a heavier sole. Before you head up a mountain, you'll want to break in your boots so that they're comfortable. You don't want your feet to hurt when you still have hours of walking ahead of you.

It's easy to spend a lot of money on hiking gear. Here are some sample prices:

Hiking boots	\$30–\$150
Zip-off pants	\$20–\$80
Hiking hat	\$15–\$40
Hydration pack	\$25–\$100

But do you really need to buy all of these things? Most people already have clothes and gear at home that will work just fine on the trail. Do you have a sturdy pair of athletic shoes? They'll serve you well on normal trails. And why not use the shorts, baseball cap, daypack, and water bottle you already have?

If you're going to do a lot of hiking, you may decide that the specialized gear is worth it. But think carefully before you buy so you make smart consumer choices.

Before you go hiking, you'll also want to get a good, small daypack that fits you well. It should be strong and waterproof. Choose one with a hip belt, padded shoulder straps, and strong zippers. Well-made school backpacks are okay to use when you're first getting started. You might also

Outdoor stores carry many different kinds of daypacks and backpacks. Try a lot on to find the one that fits you the best.

want to consider buying a **hydration pack**. A hydration pack is a backpack that includes a big pouch that you fill with water. Usually, the pouch is **insulated**, so the water stays cold. A tube runs from the pouch up to your mouth, so you can sip water whenever you want without having to stop and take out a bottle. Daypacks and backpacks come in many models and sizes, so try on several packs to find out which one is best for you.

All hikers need to be flexible and adaptable. You never know what conditions you might face on the trail. There might be a sudden downpour, the trail might disappear, or someone might get hurt. Hikers need to be prepared for all of these circumstances. Here are 10 items that hikers should always carry in their daypacks, to ensure they are ready for whatever the trail throws at them.

1. Map, guidebook, compass
2. Flashlight or headlamp
3. Extra food
4. Extra clothing
5. Rain gear, top and bottom
6. Sunscreen and sunglasses
7. First aid kit
8. Pocketknife
9. Waterproof matches
10. Water bottle and water

It's important to know how fast you hike so you can choose a trail that's a good length for you. Find a pace that you can keep up for a long time. You need to know your limits, but you should also challenge yourself. Adults hike 2 to 3 miles (3 to 5 kilometers) an hour. Kids hike about 1 to 2 miles (1.5 to 3 km) an hour. Your hiking

As you become a more experienced hiker, you'll find that you develop initiative and self-direction. Nothing is more satisfying than setting high goals for yourself and then meeting them. As you choose hikes, try to push yourself. With diligence and a good attitude, you'll find that you can accomplish even more than what you expected.

But remember, a hike's "success" can be measured in many more ways than miles covered. If you got some fresh air and exercise, if you enjoyed nature's beauty, and if you had fun with friends and family, then you had a successful hike, even if it was short.

speed will vary depending on the difficulty of the trail. Adults are often surprised by how far kids can go in one day.

To help hikers choose a trail that's right for them, some parks rate hikes by their level of difficulty. For example, an easy hike might be less than 5 miles (8 km) without much climbing. A moderate hike might be 5 to 10 miles (8 to 16 km) with some uphill hiking. And a difficult hike might be more than 10 miles (16 km) long with some challenging hills.

Just before starting up the trail, take a few minutes to gently loosen and warm up major leg muscles. Touch your toes, and stretch your thigh and calf muscles. Hikers should start slowly and end slowly. Five to 10 minutes of gentle walking at the start and end of a hike will prevent injuries and reduce muscle soreness.

CHAPTER THREE

Safety on the Trails

When you go hiking, someone in your group should carry a trail map and know how to read it.

Hiking on a trail is generally a safe activity, so long as you plan well, learn the basics, obey the rules, respect nature, and use common sense. The more you know, the safer you'll be.

Hiking with others not only makes hiking more fun, it also helps you develop a great sense of teamwork and **collaboration**. Here are some tips for enjoying hiking with others:

- Bring a new friend. It's fun to experience hiking with friends. It will give you a lot to talk about afterward.
- Work as a team. If anyone in your group is having a hard time getting up the trail, give them encouragement. You could also help them out by carrying some of their things in your pack or by offering water or a snack. If you collaborate, you will all be able to reach your goal.
- Don't whine. You know how awful it is to be around someone who complains a lot. Instead of whining if you're tired, have a snack, take a look at the view, pretend you're an animal—do anything to distract yourself, but don't whine!
- Stay together. Stay within sight or sound of your hiking group.
- Share the experience. Take photos of the hike and show them to those who came with you—and to those who wish they did! Maybe they'll join you next time.

A safe hiker learns about a trail before hiking it. Know where you were when you started the hike and where you're going. If you can read a map and know which direction you're heading, that's a big help to staying on the right trail. Tell a responsible adult where you're hiking and when you plan to return. Call this person when you return from the hike.

Stay with the group, and stay on the trail. It's tempting to explore areas off the trail. But finding your way back to the trail is not always as easy as it might seem. Bring a whistle. If you get lost or separated from the others in your group, you can blow the whistle so they can find you.

Always stay with your group when you hike.

Be sure to check the weather before you head out. Dress for the forecast, but also be prepared for changes in the weather.

Avoid getting too hot or too cold by wearing the right clothing and drinking lots of water. If you start to feel weak or dizzy, if you start shivering or sweating too much, or if you feel sick or strange in any way,

Hiking involves preparation. You need to be aware of the trail ahead of you and plan accordingly. Find out if there are any large animals or snakes where you're hiking and what to do if you see one of these creatures. You should also learn to recognize harmful plants such as poison ivy or poison oak. Know about bugs—ticks, mosquitoes, and other tiny pests—and when and where to use insect repellent.

Watch your step as you hike. Falls cause many hiking injuries. Look out for loose rocks, roots that stick out, and muddy trails. When hiking downhill, slow down and shorten your stride. Going too fast downhill can result in losing your balance and having a painful fall.

Blisters, insect bites, cuts, scratches, and sunburn are common hiking injuries. All of these can be treated if you bring a first aid kit with you on the trail. Being prepared and knowing what to do if an injury happens makes the difference between having fun on your hike and not!

tell the others in your group. These could be signs of serious illnesses such as hyperthermia (when your body gets too hot) or hypothermia (when your body gets too cold). Anyone feeling overheated should get out of the sun and be given water to drink. Once that person feels well enough, the group should take the easiest route back down the mountain. If someone can't stop shivering, wrap him or her in any extra clothes anyone has—make sure to cover the neck and the head—and get that person off the mountain and somewhere warm as quickly as possible. Being out in nature is fun, but safety must always be the first priority.

CHAPTER FOUR

Environmental Responsibilities

Reaching a spectacular viewpoint is one of the great joys of hiking.

You're a hiker because you love nature. Take good care of it. Hikers respect nature by leaving rocks, plants, and other natural objects as they found them. An old saying goes, "Take only pictures, leave only footprints." Don't litter. If you packed it in, pack it out.

When you hit the hiking trail, you must demonstrate responsibility and leadership. It is up to you to know how people can damage the wilderness and environment. When you understand the causes and effects of pollution and littering, you will begin to understand why we all need to do our part in maintaining our environment. Here are some ways to help:

- Plan ahead and prepare. If you can, avoid the crowds and hike on days and at times when there are fewer people on the trail.
- Stay on the trail. Walk in single file. If you walk off the trail, it can damage the soil and cause **erosion**.
- Dispose of waste properly. Clean up all trash and leftover food.
- Leave what you find. Admire the rocks and leaves and flowers, but leave them where they are.
- Respect wildlife. Keep your distance and don't feed animals.

Listen to nature's sounds while out on the trail: birdcalls, water bubbling over rocks, wind blowing through the trees. Avoid talking loudly or making loud noises while hiking. And leave those electronics at home. You're there to enjoy nature. Allow others to do the same.

It's also important when hiking to stay on the trail. If you walk off the trail, it can compact the dirt and kill the plants. And without plants to hold the dirt in place, it will wash away down the hillside.

Use park bathrooms before you hit the trail. Chemical toilets (or porta-potties), even clean ones, can be stinky, but use them whenever possible. During the hike, if you need to relieve yourself, do so well away from picnic areas, campsites, water sources, and the trail itself.

Properly dispose of human waste. Dig a hole 6 inches (15 centimeters) deep with your heel. Dispose of toilet paper by sealing it in a plastic bag and packing it out.

As more and more hikers head outdoors, protecting the natural areas that we visit becomes more important. The goal for hikers is "leave no trace," which means to enjoy time in nature and leave behind no signs of their visit.

Going off the trail can damage plants and cause erosion.

Trails don't just happen; they are designed and built. A trail helps hikers enjoy the beauty of nature and provides an interesting way to travel from point A to point B. Building a good trail is both an art and a science. Even after a trail is built, it will need repair and maintenance often. Forest plants grow quickly and can crowd the sides of the trail, until it becomes difficult or even impossible to hike. Erosion can also mess up a trail.

Maintaining trails is hard work. Most of it is done by **volunteers**. Take initiative and responsibility for your environment by volunteering to build or fix a trail in your area. You'll learn all about tools and trails, and you'll feel good that you've done something for the environment and for other hikers. You might want to take a leadership role and bring a group of friends on the trail to help clean up and repair it. You can become a role model who inspires others to do the same!

CHAPTER FIVE

Health Benefits

Regular physical activity such as hiking leads to a happier, healthier, and often longer life. Hiking makes the heart stronger, improves balance, and increases endurance.

Hiking builds strong muscles.

Hiking makes people healthier and happier.

Hiking has many of the same benefits as walking and running, and some special ones, too. Because every step a hiker takes along a trail is a little bit different from the previous one (uphill, downhill, over rocks), hiking gives muscles a special kind of workout.

Did you ever wonder how many calories you burn hiking? Running? How about brushing your teeth? Look at the chart below to see how many calories you burn doing different activities. This chart is for a person who weighs 100 pounds (45 kilograms). If you weigh more, you'll burn a little more. If you weigh less, you'll burn a little less.

Activity	Calories Burned Per Hour
Basketball	500
Running	450
Hiking hills	360
Dancing	300
Hiking flat trails	285
Swimming	275
Riding a bike	250
Skateboarding	230
Brushing teeth	115
Watching TV	50

Studies show that eating healthy food and taking hikes helps keep you fit. A hiker who walks 2 miles (3 km) along a relatively flat trail in an hour burns about 285 calories. Hiking with a pack increases the calories burned;

Hiking uphill is a serious workout.

More and more people are discovering the joys of hiking.

so does hiking faster and going uphill. By comparison, sitting around watching TV or playing video games burns only about 50 calories an hour. There's no question that hiking is a lot better for you than gaming, and many people say it's a lot more fun, too.

Drink lots of water when you hike.

Exercise helps keep your bones and muscles strong. And doctors have found that it lowers your chance of developing cancer, heart disease, and high blood pressure when you get older. And just as important, hiking (and other exercise) makes you feel better. It is good for the body and the mind.

You use a lot of energy when you're out on the trail, so you need to make sure you eat right. Rather than eat large meals, many hikers prefer packing a variety of healthy snacks that can be eaten throughout the day. Favorite trail foods include cheese and crackers, dried fruit, and "ants on a log" (celery spread with peanut butter and topped with raisins). Keep a few power foods (energy bars, granola bars) in your pack. If you don't eat the bars on your hike, save them for the next hike or for an emergency.

Gorp (short for "good old raisins and peanuts"), or trail mix, is the most popular snack for hikers. Making your own trail mix at home is fun, and you can add all kinds of tasty ingredients, such as almonds, coconut, dried apricots, pretzels, granola, sunflower seeds, and banana chips.

Hikers need to drink lots of water on a hike, particularly on hot days. Don't wait until you're thirsty to drink. Drink small amounts throughout the hike. Make sure you bring at least a quart of water for yourself, more for longer hikes or on a hot day. Don't plan to find water on the way. Water from streams, lakes, and rivers must be treated before drinking it.

A good way to train for hiking is to walk. Walk to school. Walk to the store. Walk up stairs instead of using the elevator. In bad weather, go for a walk at the mall or around the indoor track at a gym. Some hikers stay

Some people train for hiking by going to the gym. But there are lots of exercises you can do at home or at school that will make you stronger. Be creative and innovative as you start your training program. Here is an exercise you can use to strengthen your calf muscles, which are essential for hiking. And the best part is, you can do this exercise while sitting at your school desk:

1. Sit in an upright position, with both feet flat on the floor.
2. Slowly raise your knees up to the bottom of your desk, using your toes to push up. Make sure your toes stay on the ground.
3. You should feel your calves tense up. Once they do, slowly lower your feet back down to the ground.
4. Repeat this 50 times, and you'll be amazed at how strong your legs become in a week!

Can you think of some other ways to train for hiking?

in shape by working out on a treadmill. Some treadmills have settings that make you feel like you're walking up a trail. Whatever you do to train for your hiking adventure, be sure that you make it fun! Find what works for you, and start a training program. Remember, training takes initiative and motivation, so get out there and get going!

Begin with short hikes on flat ground. As you get more experience, increase the distance you hike and add some hills. By increasing the amount of time you spend on the trail with each new hike, you'll become a stronger hiker.

So take a break from city life. Get outside and have a good time with friends and family. Explore

Hiking is good for the body and the spirit.

wonderful new places. Enjoy the peace of nature. Hike—and keep hiking. You might just discover that hiking is your favorite outdoor sport, one that you'll enjoy for many years to come.

Glossary

collaboration (kuh-lah-buh-RAY-shun) the act of working together or cooperating

erosion (ih-RO-zhun) the process of wearing away

fleece (FLEES) a soft, lightweight fabric

hydration pack (hi-DRAY-shun PAK) a backpack with a large water pouch and a tube that runs to the hiker's mouth

insulated (IN-suh-lay-ted) covered in a way that prevents the item's contents from heating up or cooling down

terrain (tuh-RAIN) the physical features of the land

volunteers (vah-lun-TEERZ) people who do work without getting paid for it

zip-off pants (ZIP OFF PANTS) pants that can be unzipped so they become shorts

For More Information

Books

Berger, Karen. *Hiking and Backpacking.* New York: Dorling Kindersley, 2005.

Hiking. Irving, TX: Boy Scouts of America, 2002.

Loy, Jessica. *Follow the Trail: A Young Person's Guide to the Great Outdoors.* New York: Henry Holt and Co., 2003.

McKinney, John. *The Joy of Hiking: Hiking the Trailmaster Way.* Berkeley: Wilderness Press, 2005.

Web Sites

ABC-of-Hiking.com
www.abc-of-hiking.com
For all kinds of stories and advice about hiking

American Hiking Society
www.americanhiking.org
To learn how you can help protect trails

Hiking and Backpacking
www.hikingandbackpacking.com
To compare prices on gear or to find a good trail

Index

About the Author

John McKinney, "the Trailmaster," is the father of two kids who like to hike. He is also the author of *The Joy of Hiking* and about a dozen other books on hiking. Learn more about hiking on his Web site, www.thetrailmaster.com.